THE TALE OF MR. BRITTLES

DEDICATED TO MY HUSBAND, CHILDREN, AND ALL OF THOSE WHO HAVE SUPPORTED ME DURING MY CREATIVE JOURNEY.

A SPECIAL THANKS TO MY FRIEND OF MANY YEARS BLAKE MATHIAS WHO IS ALSO PURSUING HIS OWN CREATIVE JOURNEY. I'M PROUD OF YOU.

Note to Reader:

It began the way all genuine horror begins, with a cautionary tale. A warning to the children of the fate that would befall them if they were not good, if they didn't listen or if they slipped out of their homes after dark. There are monstrous entities out there, waiting, lurking, seizing the moment your child creeps out of their window and into the night. So huddle close as we begin this tale and keep a close eye on your children. You never know when Mr. Brittles might be watching.

"Mr. Brittles had a mouth,
But he had no teeth,
So poor Mr. Brittles could not eat.

Mr. Brittles was so hungry,
All he wanted was a feast,
Some delectable juicy meat,
All his to eat.

Peeking into the trap he set,
He was delighted with such a find,
A boy aged but three without sound mind,
So happy with his catch,
He squealed out with glee.

For now, he had something good to eat, you see.
Boiling the child's meat,
Finally preparing his feast,
That would transform him into a ravenous beast.

Beware of Mr. Brittles,
For he is after children like you and me.
Mean Mr. Brittles' house is a shade of brown,
If you see it,
You would surely frown,
But shush, stay quiet.
Don't make a sound,
Or he will hear you and we will be found.

If he sees you,
You'll never escape,
Forever trapped within his place,
No one will ever see you or your precious face,
Every ounce and trace of you shall be erased,
If Mr. Brittles' gets his way.

Every day I walked by the fence that surrounded Mr. Brittles' property. The iron bars were the only things that kept us safe.

We had all heard the rumors of the monstrosities that supposedly took place inside the confines of that eerie home. No flowers grew there, all the grass inside the gates appeared as a deep toxic yellow sprouting from the earth, suffocating his lawn. That horrible brown house loomed at the end of the lane like a gray storm cloud, always lurking just at the edge of a peaceful sunny sky. Those gates were all that separated us from this alleged murderer, who always sits outside in that creaky wooden rocking chair watching us.

Though we all tried, none of us could escape his sinister glare from his throne on the front porch. He always wore his green V-neck shirt and a pair of sweatpants that may have been gray at one time. When we saw him, he flashed his wicked grin and exposed his blackened smile. He had no teeth as far as I could tell, which is why every time he grinned at me, I stood frozen, paralyzed by fear. My legs quaked, and I could feel my heart speeding up, worried it may shatter inside my ribcage.

He would lean forward like a feral cat stalking its next meal, every time a kid ventured too close to the gate.

All the children walked in tight groups, following the instructions from their parents. If one child straggled behind, he may slink from his porch and drag them inside to his domain. Boiling their bones until the meat slipped from them, just like the rumors had forewarned.

Mr. Brittles, presenting himself as a feeble old man, also gave the ominous feeling of being something otherworldly. Something much more sinister than a simple mortal man.

He watched from his bleak perch as all the school kids walked to the bus stop. He was always there, waiting and watching menacingly. Those who didn't believe the stories would always taunt him to see his reaction.

"Get off of that porch old man!"

"Yeah, c'mon you toothless son of a bitch!"

"Nasty old geezer!"

"What are you staring at fuckface?! Why don't you come down here and do something?"

"Your wrinkly old ass can't even get out of your chair!"

I overheard Jake Westford and Dylan Stolly shouting toward him on that winter morning. While brave, they were also fools. I watched in horror as he lunged forward in his chair, licking his lips, enticed by their closeness to his gate.

A shiver crept up my spine as I worried that one day Mr. Brittles might leap from that porch, dash across the yard and yank one of us over the gate, dragging us down to his cellar.

Thankfully, since the authorities deemed him unfit for society, they had chained the gate to prevent him from leaving his home without a chaperone. I pulled tightly onto the steel chains that locked his property, examining them to make sure they were secure. We were all four chains and a padlock away from becoming the rumored cannibals' next meal.

My little brother, Jack, watched Dylan and Jake as I held his hand. He stood next to me, waiting for me to take him to the bus stop. Something about today felt different. This time when I felt Mr. Brittles glaring at me, I had looked back at him. The air felt heavier and crisper than usual for fall.

Our eyes met for a moment, and I couldn't force myself to move my legs or look away, no matter how much I wanted to.

Jake and Dylan glanced in our direction, and Mr. Brittles shifted his glare to them, and I felt as if I could breathe again. I didn't hesitate a second longer. His cold eyes had sent goosebumps scurrying across my skin. Pulling my little brother along, we started down the sidewalk past the gate to the bus stop.

I rolled my eyes as I stormed past them, dragging Jack along. This was a daily thing, nothing unusual for these two.

"Ignore them, Jack. Hurry, we're going to be late getting to the bus stop."

Both of us looked over our shoulders, as Mr. Brittles just grinned at the boys; he never said a word. He sat patiently in his rocking chair, taking their insults, waiting and watching for one of them to get brave enough to cross over the gate into his yard.

"Why do they tease him?" Jack asked as he finally turned his head away and looked up at me for answers.

I had often wondered the same thing myself. I assumed they had heard the cautionary tale surrounding him and the property. Our parents had told it to us when we first moved here nearly a year ago.

Our grandmother had passed the tale down to our mother and then to us. The Tale of Mr. Brittles was common knowledge among the elders of the town, and I assumed, like my mother, that they too had passed it down the line. Generation to generation, to keep us all fearful of the man who lived at the end of the street.

Mr. Brittles, according to my mother, she believed him to be this ancient otherworldly being, something that existed before the town of Robin's Hollow, and it would still exist long after the town decayed. Even when she had been a kid herself, he sat outside on that porch trapped by the iron gates.

He never seemed to grow old, his appearance staying the same year after year. No matter how much time passed or how many children grew into adults. Mr. Brittles stayed the same, and as always, rocked on his front porch, watching and waiting.

She used to tell me and Jack that a witch had enchanted the gates before they built the town and that if we stayed outside the gates, Mr. Brittles couldn't harm us.

"As long as you never step inside, you will be safe." Mother would say while me and Jack sat there listening to her stories.

"What happens if we go inside?" Jack had wondered as curiosity brimmed from his eyes.

When I had been his age, my mind was just as inquisitive. He got his questions from our grandmother, a trait that he and I had inherited. The only trait that seemed to remain of her after she'd passed away.

Jack reminded me so much of her and I missed her terribly.

"If that happened, then mean Mr. Brittles will gobble you up. Devour your very skin from your bones and cook your little toes into his soup." Mother warned playfully as she nibbled at Jack's feet, and he giggled.

"Seriously, what will happen?" I had asked, eager for the answer to the gnawing question that ate away at my mind.

Her beautiful brown eyes met mine as she continued tickling Jack, who rolled around on the bed, his laughter spilling out of him like water from a fountain. He always had that infectious life filling laughter. The kind that made everyone else laugh along with him.

"Cat, Jack, if you two ever find yourself on his property for any reason, whether by fate or by accident, do not let him catch you. Supposedly, a group of seniors from Robin's Hollow many years ago, when your grandmother had been a young girl, jumped the gate to go snooping around Mr. Brittles property. Back then, Robins Hollow had just started growing. All the stores and businesses that exist now didn't exist back then. Mr. Brittles hasn't changed at all from then, but he supposedly had a diamond mine underneath his home. When the city offered to buy his property, he had refused them." My mother retrieved her coffee from the nightstand table, taking a big gulp of it before she continued.

Jack's eyelids were becoming heavy, but I had been wide awake. My brain listening to every word, clinging, and clamoring for more history of the town and my grandmother's adventures growing up here.

"Your great, great, grandfather had been the councilman that he had refused and upon sharing this information at home with his family. His wife and your grandmother sprinkled it throughout the town. Soon the town had been abuzz with the rumor, and everyone wanted to get their hands on a genuine diamond. The seniors had hoped that maybe they'd find one by digging deep enough in his backyard. The legend goes that all those uninvited who crossed over his gate vanished. Not a trace of them, as if they had never existed at all. With so many newcomers to the town, memories of them rapidly faded."

Jack had fallen asleep, but I had been wide awake listening intently to my mother's bedtime tale.

The moonlight pouring in from outside made the setting that much more eerie, and I trembled as she wrapped me up tightly in a blanket.

After another sip of coffee, she continued.

"Your grandmother told me that out of the entire class, only four seniors came back from his house that night. Once they came back, however, they were not the same. They had witnessed horrible things, so awful they wouldn't share the details. Two of the girls that came back immediately withdrew from Robin's Hollow Highschool and moved out of the town with their families. The two boys stayed in town but refused to talk to the police about anything they had witnessed or what had happened to the rest of the class. However, they did share with their classmates that the only way they survived was because they didn't get caught. Unlike many other seniors, who have been missing for over three decades. So truthfully, no one knows what really happened to those kids. But my mother warned me when I was a little girl never to go near those gates. I don't want you or Jack playing around there, either." She had finished her tale, but it had sent my mind racing.

She tucked me into bed, gave me a kiss on the forehead, and then exited my room.

Now, that day feels like a foggy, clouded dream, as it has been a year since we have lived in Robin's Hollow.

We had been so happy when we first moved here that this memory made my heart ache with pain as I remembered, not long after that our beloved grandmother had passed away. Leaving our mother in a state of sadness, we feared she may never recover from.

Still, we all lived peacefully alongside Mr. Brittles, yet there were some like Jake and Dylan who sought to disrupt the peace by tormenting the old man. Eager to tempt him and see if the cautionary tale were true, or if it was all superstitious folklore.

"Jack, they're just being stupid. Don't pay any attention to them. C'mon let's get to the bus. Hurry, we're going to miss it." I reassured him as I patted his head.

We ran to the bus stop and boarded the bus. Jake and Dylan trailed behind, still yelling insults at the old man.

"I want to be brave like them when I grow up." Jack stated as he walked down the aisle of the bus before sitting down in a nearby window seat.

I scooted in next to him, wrapping my arm around his shoulder and petting his hair down.

I adored my little brother. He was our entire world, mine included, since he had been born. My whole family felt as if Jack had completed us. Our trio of mom, dad and I became a quartet when Jack was born.

"One for each of us." I remembered hearing my parents saying to each other when they brought Jack home from the hospital.

My father, he had always wanted a son and mom had always wanted a girl. Now that they had Jack, they had their idea of a perfect family. Naturally, I became closer with mom and Jack never left our dad's side.

"Jack, I already told you they're just being stupid boys. They are being mean to poor Mr. Brittles. He might be scary but, he's still a person with feelings. I am sure their remarks are hurtful to him. Besides, rumors and stories are just that. Just fiction like in the books you read at school. There is no proof what the tale says is real or not. No records proving any of it really happened." I tell him as the bus starts up.

Dylan and Jake pile onto the bus, still laughing from their earlier torments.

I roll my eyes as they walk past, shooting an annoyed glance at them.

"Hi Cat." Jake says as he walks by our seat. I don't even acknowledge him or give him a response.

I keep my head turned toward Jack, keeping my eyes on his face.

"Then why do they keep bothering him?" Jack asks me, as he fidgets with a toy robot, pulling it from his pocket.

"Some people are just bullies. When you grow up, you are going to be better than them, okay? You don't want to be like them. They might seem brave, but it's never okay to pick on the elderly. It's up to us to take care of our elders and our parent's when they get old. Imagine if Mr. Brittles had been our grandfather, and some teens were tormenting him. How upset it would make you? What they do is not okay at all." I say reassuring him, not wanting my little brother to get the wrong idea that their behavior was acceptable.

Though, we didn't know Mr. Brittles personally. Our grandmother had always encouraged us to be polite to the old man, especially since he never came close to the gate or off his porch when we walked by. I remembered asking her and our parents about him often.

"If he was my grandpa, I'd beat them up!" Jack said as he played with the robot, shooting it up in the air and shaking it about as if it had laser beams for eyes.

I laughed in response, and he began giggling too. I turned away from Jack and glanced around the bus. Kids were laughing and talking, most played with their cellphones. I watched enviously; I had asked for a phone for my birthday. Though Dad insisted that a "fourteen-year-old girl didn't need a cell phone" when I had asked him.

I couldn't help it. Everyone else around my age had one. I wanted one too, so that for once I could feel as if I fit in with everyone.

Besides, the cellphones were the newest thing. They had just come to the area, and everyone had one. They came in all shapes and colors, some flipped sideways, others flipped open vertically.

Some girls in my class had decorated their phones with stickers or charms. My best friend, Megan Philmore; had one. She had moved here along with her brother Devan about the same time we did, but Devan was much older than us.

I watched eagerly as the bus pulled up to Megan's stop; she lived with her grandma instead of with Devan and their dad.

She hated her dad's new wife Marissa, and had moved out with her grandma the second she moved in. I could tell she was upset when she stomped up onto the bus. Her puffy blue eyes gave away that she had been crying, along with the rosy blush on her chubby cheeks. She brushed her brunette hair back from her face as she flopped down in the seat across from me. Her plaid shirt nearly tearing from catching the zipper of her backpack.

"What's wrong, Megan?" I ask her while turning to face her. Swinging my legs out towards the aisle.

"I hate him."

"Who?"

"My dad." She responds as she wipes her eyes with her sleeve.

"Woah, what happened?" I ask.

"He wants me to move back in with him, Devan, and Marissa. He threatened to come to my granny's and drag me out of the house kicking and screaming. He said no matter what, I had to come home and make the best of things, since Marissa is part of the family now. Whether I like it or not, I wish he never met her." She sobbed, holding her face in her hands.

Megan's dad wasn't a very kind man. He had spent years controlling her and her mother, often getting aggressive with them. Megan once told me he had locked her in her room for hours and refused to let her out. She had to pee in the trash can in the corner of her room, because he had refused to let her out or feed her. She banged and clawed at her door until her fingernails broke and bled.

Her voice was hoarse from the hours spent pleading and screaming for mercy. She stayed locked inside her room for nearly a week until her mother finally returned from her business trip. When her mother discovered what happened, she immediately took Megan to her grandmother's house.

Her mother had separated from her father that very night, refusing to leave Megan's side. No longer able to tolerate her husband's excessive drinking or abusive behavior.

All had been going well until last month. Since her mother died unexpectedly in a car accident at the end of the lane, merely inches from Mr. Brittles' iron gates. He was watching from his rocking chair as the ambulance arrived on scene, according to what Megan told me.

Presumably he was the only witness to the brutal accident, and thanks to him, emergency services had gotten there fast enough to save Megan's infant sister, who had been in the backseat. But not fast enough to save her mother.

It was around that time that my view of Mr. Brittles had changed. He couldn't be the murderous cannibal the rumors proclaimed him to be and call the police, seeking to help a dying woman in a car accident. He had come from his porch that day and stood by his gates, yelling for help for her mother, all while calling the police many times from his cellphone.

There were rumors it was Marissa's car who had collided with her mother and then sped off before the police arrived on the scene.

As soon as her mother separated from him, he began dating Marissa publicly. Their divorce wasn't final, and they were working through custody issues when the accident happened.

Since her mother believed that her husband was having an affair with Marissa, she was prepared to win custody of the three children. Her death brought the case to a swift end.

Though no one knew for sure, we all suspected Marissa. It had been a hit-and-run accident, and the other car hadn't been on scene when the police arrived. Mr. Brittles walked down to his gate and talked to the police officers when it happened, informing them of the details of the accident.

His testimony caused Marissa to become the prime suspect. However, Megan's father provided a perfect alibi.

I had seen him along with my family that morning. He didn't look sinister at all. Maybe a little disheveled, but he seemed just as upset as the rest of us were from the car accident. He was almost manic describing the way the metal caved in around Megan's mother.

He almost seemed genuinely concerned until his worry transformed into fascination as he began smiling. Once he realized he broke character, he went back to the caring old man he portrayed in the beginning.

My family and I were all huddled together in our pajamas on that early fall morning.

The entire neighborhood emptied from their houses, pouring out into their yards, and crowded around the scene. All the people around stood staring in silence.

Upon hearing the commotion, Megan's grandmother hobbled down the street in her loungewear. When she arrived at the scene, Megan's grandmother recognized the car and threw her cane to the ground, rushing to make sure everyone was okay.

Upon seeing just how bad the damage was, she wailed in such horrific screams that I had nightmares for weeks after it. Her screams branded into my brain like a hot poker, forever echoing in my dreams.

My mother had rushed to Megan's side, cradling her in her arms and turning her face away from the scene as she screamed and cried too.

"You don't need to see this, Megan." She kept repeating as Megan struggled to turn back toward the scene of the accident. She held her close, refusing to let her look. That had been the only time I had ever seen genuine fear in my mother's eyes.

My father had also sprung into action, grabbing me and my brother, rushing us back inside and closing the door.

"Stay inside. I am going back out to check on your mother and Megan. Do not come back outside under any circumstances. Do you hear me, Catherine? No matter what. You and Jack stay inside." He had firmly shut the door, leaving us to view the catastrophe happening outside our living room window.

We watched as he ran back out to help our mother and Megan, comforting them both.

It took over an hour for Megan's dad to arrive, and when he did, he was with Marissa. I easily could tell he was drunk upon his arrival, as he staggered about, barely able to stand. Marissa stayed inside his car, not even stepping out to check on Megan or her grandmother.

Her grandmother sat destroyed in the middle of the street in her nightgown, covered in her mother's blood. Though the glass of the window had muted it, I could still see the anguish stretched across her wrinkled face.

Losing her mother had devastated Megan, and the moment her father heard of the accident he began making demands of Megan's grandmother that Megan return home to him immediately. Megan refused to go back to her abusive dad and wanted instead to stay with her grandmother. This hadn't been the first time he had threatened her.

After recalling this terrible memory, I reached over, grabbing Megan's hand in mine to comfort her.

"Meg," I say, looking at her. "Don't listen to your dad. He's probably just drunk, and Marissa put him up to calling. He's just talking out of his ass; it probably doesn't mean anything."

The profanity being something I had picked up from school. It was new to me. I just recently started using swear words. I hoped Jack didn't hear me, because he'd tell our parents and I'd get into trouble.

We weren't allowed to use swear words at home, but I often did at school or on the bus when Jack wasn't paying attention.

Releasing her hand, I glanced over my shoulder at Jack. He sat there humming happily, staring out the window as the bus passed by the gas station. We were close to the school, and I sighed in relief, hoping the day would pass quickly.

Turning back toward Megan, she still sat there crying, and I continued trying to comfort her until we got off the bus. Once we went into the school, the day passed by fast.

I hated the boring assignments; the teachers droning on and on with useless knowledge. Things I believed I would never use once I became an adult. I hated all my classes this year, and often felt the content was too easy or not challenging enough for me. I'd always breezed through my classes. Elementary school had been so easy for me, I'd skipped about a couple of grades testing out of them.

Luckily, Hollow High accepted me into their sophomore class with no issues. I blended in easily with the rest of the sophomore girls, though I often felt like I didn't belong. Though in their eyes, I became labeled as a "geek" or a "freak."

I never made friends easily after that, aside from Megan. But, for me, that was okay. Megan made up for all the missing friends I could've had. She had the latest gossip and knew about all the drama going on in the sophomore classes. My days with her never felt boring.

After that day, my life would never have the peace or tranquility of being boring ever again. Nothing would ever be the same. I would never step foot inside of Hollow High ever again.

The town of Robin's Hollow will forever be marked by the darkest tragedy to befall the town in over twenty years.

I had assumed my parents had picked Jack up from school when he didn't get on the bus that afternoon. Megan and I watched as Bluebird Elementary's students and staff poured out of the doors.

We kept waiting for Jack to come out of the school and board onto the bus, but after several minutes I had this sinking feeling in the pit of my stomach. I couldn't explain it, but I knew something had happened to Jack.

"Where's Jack?" Megan asked me, breathing on the window, drawing shapes in the stain left behind from her breath. I searched the crowd's faces, eager to see Jack's blonde hair bouncing along with his neon green backpack in tow. To me, his backpack looked hideous, but he loved it when Dad brought it home for him.

I didn't answer her as my thoughts drifted to the day he had received that ugly green backpack.

"It's my favorite color!" He proclaimed as he swirled the backpack in the air, dancing about in his bunny pajamas.

Seeing him that happy had made me feel envious. Dad barely noticed me or brought me anything special home, like he always did for Jack.

"You don't even know what color it is!" I called out to him as I stormed down the hallway toward his room.

"Yes, I do sissy!" He argued back with me, sticking his tongue out.

"Well, what color *is* it, then?" I asked as I crossed my arms over my chest, leaning against the doorway of his room staring in at him.

"It's… it's…" His voice trailed off, and I instantly knew I had won.

"See? Told you, you didn't know what color it was!" I teased, laughing at him, as I watched his face grow red and he puffed his cheeks.

That was Jack. In the instant he was mad, he immediately got over it. I secretly wished I had inherited that from our dad, but the only thing I had inherited from him were his espresso eyes. The same brown eyes his mother, our grandmother, had passed down the line to him.

"I don't care. I still love it. I love everything Dad gets me, *you're* just jealous!"

"I am not jealous. Besides, who would want a hideous green backpack like that, anyway?" I lied to Jack; I had been jealous.

Dad and I weren't close, like my mother and I. Mom and I made cookies, laughed, shopped together and we talked about everything. When our dad got home, he shot an occasional glance in my direction. A wave or sometimes a nod, but we didn't talk to each other much. When we talked, it was more like commenting on his and Jack's conversation pieces, adding our thoughts to an already happening conversation. I wanted the connection Jack had with Dad.

So, anytime Dad doted on Jack, I felt envious because I felt like he and I were strangers towards each other.

"Helloooo. Earth to Cat! Are you even listening to me?" Megan asked, forcing me out of my daydream.

"Yeah, sorry. I was just thinking of Jack and that ugly green backpack he's always toting around. Have you seen him yet? Usually, he's on the bus by now…" I answered, as I began biting my nails.

"No eyes on Captain Jack yet. I wonder what's taking him so long?" Megan asked, looking up from her phone.

But now, as the crowd dwindled down to just a few teachers and even fewer students trickling out of the school. I held my breath, waiting for Jack. When the bus pulled out of the parking lot without him, my mind racing not knowing what could have happened.

I wanted nothing more than to see Jack.

"I hope our parents picked him up." I said, trying to reassure myself.

The worry in her eyes intensified my own. I assumed Megan also felt something was awry by the way she looked at me.

"They probably did. You know how your dad is. He always randomly picks Jack up without telling you." She assured me as she twirled her hair, looking at Jake as he strutted past her.

"Hi Megan." Jake said, flashing her a toothy smile, dropping onto the seat in front of us.

"You two are gross." I say as I continue to stare out the window.

"Don't be mean, Cat. I'm sorry about her. Her parents picked up her little brother and not her so she's in a crabby mood." Megan told him, as I shook my head at her.

"Moody Catherine; sounds like another typical day." Dylan commented as he sat down beside of Jake.

The two of them twisted their heads and bodies to face us. I just ignored them as Meg and Jake talked about the upcoming school dance.

"You want to go to the dance, Cat?" Dylan asked me. I DEFINITELY DO NOT want to go with him.

Megan had a huge crush on Jake, and I knew if I said no, that most likely meant she wouldn't be able to go.

She looked over at me, nudging me with her arm eagerly. I shot a piercing glare in her direction. She ignored it and continued nudging me. Jake and Dylan also both stared at me, awaiting an answer.

"I'll think about it." I sighed as Dylan grinned from ear to ear. He gave Jake a high five and a fist bump and I felt annoyed already.

"Thank you." Megan mouthed to me in a quiet whisper as I overheard Jake ask her to go with him. She squealed in delight, and I wished the bus ride was over already.

The moment I got home; I knew something was wrong. I entered the house to see my parents without Jack. When I made a comment about assuming they had picked him up early and after they told me they hadn't and that they thought he had been with me on the bus. I knew that the light of our world, my sweet little brother Jack, had disappeared.

My mom, becoming frantic, called Bluebird Elementary, looking for him while my dad rushed out of the house, grabbing his keys and coat. I trailed behind, determined to find Jack.

We hopped into the car and drove throughout the neighborhood shouting and looking for him.

"JACK!" I screamed out.

"JACK!"

"SON, WHERE ARE YOU?"

"SON, IF YOU CAN HEAR ME ANSWER ME!" Dad yelled out the window, as he ran through every red light as he put his emergency flashers on. I had never seen my dad cry before, but at that moment, he did. Tears welled in his eyes, as he grew more panicked as he yelled.

"JACK, PLEASE ANSWER US!"

"JACK PLEASE! COME ON JACK, ANSWER US!" I called out. My voice becoming strained as I began coughing. My dad drove even faster. He hollered his name out the window at every stop.

"Jack, where are you?" I called out the window as we passed the gas station.

"Did he get on the bus with you?" My dad questioned me as he swerved the car around.

"Dad, please slow down!" I cried out, trembling, as we narrowly missed an oncoming vehicle.

"Answer me, Catherine! Did he get on the bus with you this morning!?" He shouted at me. I watched, terrified, as he jerked the wheel around, driving like a maniac down the highway.

We were now on the outside of Robin's Hollow, heading toward Crowgrove County. My eyes scanned the overgrown fields, worrying that Jack could've wondered away from school.

"Yes dad. We sat together this morning while I talked to Meg. She sat across from us." I answered, squinting my eyes as I stared into the far away tree line.

For a second, I could've sworn I seen Mr. Brittles ominous grin, and ever-watchful eyes peering at me from the shadows of the trees.

Then I blinked, and he was gone. I knew then it had to be my imagination.

You are probably hallucinating cause you're so worried about Jack. Where on Earth could he be? I must think. Someone must know where he is or seen something. Maybe someone snatched him from school. God, I don't even want to think about that.

"Where was Jack while you were talking with Meg?" He asked me again, his foot burying the pedal.

I watched from the passenger seat as his speedometer went past the 60-mark, 70 mark and traveling toward 80mph. His voice freed me from my thoughts, and I answered him.

"He was with me. I promise he was with me, Dad. We were sitting together. I was sitting at the edge of the seat with my legs in the aisle. He never went past me. I promise, he was sitting right beside me." I answered, noticing how dark the sky had turned. Hours must have passed, though it felt like mere minutes to me.

"Is there anywhere you think he might be, Cat?" my father asked as he turned into *Crowgrove County Playground,* our car nearly smashing the wooden sign as he swerved past it.

"No dad. I don't know." I looked toward the empty playground, no one there besides my dad and me. The car sits idling in the parking lot, as his lights shined onto the playground equipment.

Darkness suffocated the remaining daylight as the moon began its ascension into the sky, and the world around me felt as if it had an ominous glow from the approaching dusk. Grey storm clouds filled the sky, and I trembled at the sound of thunder.

"Dammit, Catherine! Use your brain and think!" He shouted at me, causing me to be startled and spilling my drink all over my lap. He immediately reached past me toward the glove box, opening it and shoving the napkins inside into my hands.

"Dad, I don't know." I whimper, wiping up the spilled juice from my jeans. Scrubbing vigorously with the napkins, trying not to cry. My mind raced to thoughts of Jack and his smile flashed into my brain. I wondered if I would ever see his smile again.

Swallowing back my fear, I glanced over at my dad. He pressed his head against the steering wheel, wet tears pouring down his cheeks. The air inside the car felt heavy, as if weights bore down on us.

My heartbeat thumped inside of my chest, and I felt like I couldn't breathe. I felt like my head sunk beneath the water of an endless ocean and, despite my best attempts, I was drowning. Sinking to the bottom of the ocean's darkest depths, never to be found. Until thousands of years passed, and the ocean dried up. Only then, my corpse would resurface after being fossilized by the earth.

Once we both calmed down, my dad pulled out of the parking lot and continued searching. We both sat in silence as tears poured from our eyes.

At this moment, we had something in common for once. We were both imprisoned in our own minds, suffering from our own forms of guilt and regret. We had searched everywhere for Jack yet; he was nowhere to be found.

It was as if the heavens that blessed us to have him swooped down and swallowed him, with no trace of him left behind.

That night, my father drove to the three surrounding counties, Crowgrove County, Osprey Peak, and Macaw Hill. Our voices screeched out into the night, repeatedly calling his name until finally the realization set in that he wasn't going to be found tonight.

When we returned home, the Robin's Hollow Police Department's cars littered our driveway like horrible gnome decorations that our neighbors had on their lawn across the street. The red and blue shining lights pierced the darkness of the night sky.

Our neighbors' porch lights illuminated some of their worried and horrified expressions as they stood outside in their yards watching our tragedy unfold before them.

I see some of our neighbors, the ones that were not standing outside. I watched as they opened their curtains and peered out their windows with curiosity splattered across their faces. Their gazes and stares meeting mine as we drove past them. Pulling into the driveway, I immediately took off my seatbelt and opened the door.

The moment my feet touched the pavement, I ran inside and didn't look back. Long before my dad could even cut off the car. I met the sheriff and deputy at the door as I pushed past them, bursting into the living room and collapsing onto the couch next to my mother.

She sat on the couch; her face drained of all color.

Her eyes were red, and her hair hung in a blond tangled mess over her shoulders. She still wore her flower dress from that afternoon. I could tell that she hadn't even had the energy to change clothes before the officers came. We could see the hurt in her green eyes, and we knew instantly he was still missing. Her eyes were tired, red, and swollen as she held my hand in hers.

The days that followed blended together. We confined ourselves to our rooms as much as possible. There were no more movie nights, no family game nights, no hot dinners or breakfasts aside from what I could microwave since mom stopped cooking. For a while, the color from our world felt as if it had dissipated and all that remained was gray.

I remained hopeful that despite the tragedy plaguing our lives that one day things would return to normal and that Jack's laughter would once again fill our home.

I didn't go to school anymore. My mother signed a leave of absence form stating a "temporary leave of absence because of a family emergency" was necessary.

But I knew I would never go back to Hollow High. Everyone knew what had happened to Jack, that he was missing, and gazed upon me with pity. Some older, more spiteful students filled the halls with rumors and whispers that I had done something to Jack.

Being the weird kid, it was easy to cast blame on me, even though anyone that knows me knows I would never hurt Jack. I adored him as much as my parents. He was the light of my life, even though I never got the chance to tell him.

Neither of my parents went to work or spoke to each other. We walked around one another as if we were undead zombies, moping through the motions while time continued normally outside of our existence.

We strolled through the corridors of the house in our empty, rotting bodies. Clinging to the hope that one day, our lives would return to normal or, like the zombies, hoped for a cure to be created.

However, unlike them, I knew we couldn't go on living this way. I could feel the shift, the cracking of our family. It would soon devour us, and none of us would escape this unscathed.

I wasn't even acknowledged as they strolled past me, not speaking to me, just retrieving something to eat from the pantry or walking past to go to the bathroom. Without Jack, the house felt dead, rotting in the decay of our shattered hearts.

There had been a brief time before Jack had been born, when my parents and I had done things together. We would sometimes cuddle or watch movies; we'd have pillow fights or read stories late into the night by candlelight. Sometimes, we would hide under blankets together, making shadow puppets with a flashlight on the ceiling.

The moment Jack entered our world, the old world had ceased to exist. I grew older, and my parents' attention shifted to Jack. I never envied that part of my life though because I got to share those moments with him. I relived my entire childhood all over again as we played together, had pillow fights, we watched all my favorite movies.

My parents would serenade each other, as they danced in the kitchen while preparing our meals. With Jack came an energy and a light in our world that we didn't know we had been missing. But now that he was gone, the time before he existed felt like a far-off distant dream. A memory from a past life.

My early childhood memories with my parents felt like I had rewritten them with Jack as I tried to share all I had experienced over again with him. His laughter had been infectious and often we'd all four burst into fits of laughter together. Rolling around together in a room filled with mattresses and blankets, where *Fort Zerona* once stood.

We named it after the ancient city that our parents had told us stories about.

Now a gloomy silence filled the air of our home, trapping us in the haunting memory of his disappearance. It wasn't long after that everything fell apart.

My parents began talking, but the talking turned into arguments, slamming doors, and the destruction of anything within reaching distance. I lived with them, but I was no longer their daughter. I was the shadow that they felt invaded their home.

They blamed me for Jack being gone, even though I had nothing to do with it. They looked at me with disgust in their eyes and spoke hateful words to me that used to not even exist in their vocabulary.

I grew to resent them, just as they resented me. I hated myself too and blamed myself for Jack being gone just as much as they did. For a while, I wanted to run away and go anywhere else besides home.

Within eight weeks, I had returned to school, but it felt as if a decade had passed since Jack had gone missing. I had remained hopeful returning to Hollow High would bring me some type of happiness. Instead, the hurt continued.

I couldn't walk down the hallway without being stared at or whispered about. Even Meg seemed distant, though I needed her support. In the darkest part of my loneliness, something else formed inside of me.

It felt like something new had chosen me and I would be its keeper. I became angrier, dark thoughts invading my mind. Causing me to feel drained and ravenous with rage.

Every day I walked by Mr. Brittles house, and every day it loomed over me. Sometimes I'd stop outside and peer over at it. The air had shifted around it since Jack's disappearance, almost as if it held some secret of him within. Other times, I felt as if the house's aura was beckoning me, inviting me inside.

I thought often of the story my mother had told me about the seniors, and I often pictured myself going over those gates and stomping into Mr. Brittles' territory. After the police questioned him about Jack's disappearance, he hadn't been coming outside as often. He peeked from the safety of his window out at everyone, rather than from his rocking chair.

Still, something felt odd about that sinister brown house and the man that lived inside.

On my evening walk home from the bus stop, I heard a voice calling out to me from the brown house as I walked by his gate, noticing that the chains were gone.

"Catherine Rhodes." The voice chanted my name, and I felt mesmerized by the unlocked gate as that haunting poem creeped into my mind yet again. My brother wasn't the only one who had gone missing.

Dozens of kids from Crowgrove County and Osprey Peak also disappeared mysteriously, following Jack's disappearance. Though before this day, I'd never truly believed the rumors circling the old man.

But I couldn't deny the overwhelming feeling in my gut I got as I stared up at the black smoke pouring out of his chimney. I could no longer ignore the smell of burning flesh and charcoal that seemed to emanate from that house.

The voice grew louder inside my head, beckoning to me like a beacon of light in the night for the sailors at sea.

My parents and I searched all over town, and everyone had come out to look for Jack. Except for Mr. Brittles, who had curiously watched from the safety of his front porch.

It was one of the few times I'd seen him standing against a banister with his mouth closed and not smiling. In his eyes reflected something I hadn't seen before, worry. He looked worried, and I suspected he knew something or could have something to do with Jack's disappearance.

Later that night, I left my parents' house meeting up with Megan. I had convinced her of my suspicions earlier at school. Reluctantly, she agreed to come with me to investigate.

My parents hadn't even noticed that I left since they were too busy bickering with each other.

I encouraged Megan to follow me as we began our search. Megan and I gripped our flashlights as we called out for Jack.

Mr. Brittles turned and went inside of his house, shutting the door so hard, it startled us from the street. We had never seen him outside at night before. However, tonight it was as if he had been looking for us. Waiting for us to come down the lane with our flashlights.

I wondered if Megan thought the same thing, because she glanced at me with a puzzled look on her face and whispered.

"Do you think he's responsible for what happened to Jack?" she questioned, as we stopped mere inches from the gate I now knew had been unlocked. The only barrier between our world and his no longer existed. I had told Megan about the unlocked gate earlier and that the chains, along with the padlock, were gone. She shined her flashlight on the gate, revealing that the chains were still there and so was the padlock.

Nothing had changed, except despite how many times I blinked my eyes, there were no chains or lock that I could see. However, Megan insisted they were there. She even lifted them up, shining her flashlight on it to show me. But I still didn't see anything there. I questioned my sanity as I watched Megan flailing her hands through the void.

Am I losing my mind? Megan keeps saying the gate's still locked up, but I haven't seen the chains since this afternoon. What is wrong with me? Maybe I'm going crazy. Losing Jack is making me feel insane. Why can't I see them? Why are they not there when I look? I don't understand any of this.

"I don't know anything anymore. I mean, I know all the stories, but with Jack missing, it's hard not to suspect him. He's been acting different since the disappearance." I say. I rub my eyes vigorously, hoping the chains will reappear in my vision again.

They do not.

"Maybe you should tell your parents about it and the police. They can search his place if they think he might have something to do with Jack going missing."

She assured me as she locked her arms with mine, trembling from the cold winter air.

I didn't look at her. My gaze stayed focused on the smoke. I could still see it rising from his chimney, and as the burned aroma returned, I could feel my nostrils stinging.

"The police have already interviewed him and cleared him as a suspect." I whisper back to her.

My father had demanded the police question him, given all the rumors we had heard about Mr. Brittles. My father would not let the rumors go. He got drunk, becoming belligerent and storming down to the Robin's Hollow Police Department.

My father had been relentless in his pursuit of justice for Jack. Sheriff Michael Waters finally went out to interview Mr. Brittles and when my father learned they had cleared him of being a suspect.

He remained in his drunken stupor at home.
"Really? Wow! I didn't know that. I am so sorry about Jack. I really hope they find him, Cat." She says to me as she brushes the snowflakes from her coat with her gloves.

Winter drew closer, and it felt as if an eternity had passed between Megan and me since he went missing.

"Hey Cat, are you still going with Dylan to the dance? Jake and I want to go." She says as we linger at Mr. Brittle's gates.

My eyes shift to her face, breaking away from the smoke. I notice how close she is standing next to me.

"Seriously, Meg, is that all you can think about right now?" I ask her as I cross my arms over my chest.

"What's wrong with it?"

"Nothing is wrong with it, but Jack is missing." I say, barely able to vocalize the words out loud.

My heart shatters the moment I croak out his name. The pain bursts from inside of me all at once, sending daggers through my veins.

"Look Cat, I understand that, and it sucks so bad for you and your family. But we must think about ourselves, too." She says as she puts her hands on my cheeks, lifting my face to look at her.

I jerk away from her and take a step back.
"You're unbelievable Megan. All you care about is yourself. My brother is missing, and I don't care about some stupid fucking dance. You just want me to go, so you can make out with Jake all night long. You don't care about me or what I am going through at all!" I scream at her, unable to fight the tears any longer.

All the rage, hurt, and fear I had been bottling up is now pouring out of me. I no longer can contain myself as I scream at her.

"Catherine! That is so not true! But we all can't just give up our lives and keep looking for Jack. I know you love him and he's your brother. But we must go back to *our* lives now. We can't just give up living because he *might* be dead." She says to me.

I don't think I only react.

I smack her. Hard across the face, and I know in this moment our friendship is over. She bursts into tears as she presses her hand to her cheek. Her face reads confusion and shock. I am also shocked. I couldn't believe I'd just slapped my best friend.

Her eyes looking into mine with such defeat, as she turns away from me.

"Megan please! Wait, Megan! Dammit, I am sorry!" I plead with her as she runs away from me. Megan doesn't stop.

In fact, she runs faster and heads farther away from me. I drop to my knees as the snow falls around me, realizing I am all alone now.

I look back up to the black chimney, smoke sputtering into the sky, and from my knees I can see there in the window. The light inside illuminates a familiar hideous green hue. My body tenses, and I blink several times, making sure that what I am seeing is real.

There in the attic of Mr. Brittles' house, sitting against a chair arm, pressed up by the corner of the window, was Jack's backpack. I get to my feet and run home to alert my parents to tell them what I had just seen in his attic window.

Upon my arrival home, my parents are still engaged from their argument earlier.

I storm into the house, not closing the door behind me, letting the cold air follow me inside.

"Mom, Dad, I saw Jack's backpack." I say, barely able to catch my breath.

"Where?" my dad asked as he rushes to put on his coat by the door.

He doesn't hesitate, breaking off his argument with my mother. It's the first time in weeks he's spoken to me.

"Oh my gosh honey, where?" My mom asks immediately after my dad.

She stays sitting at the table, her eyes never leaving her meeting planner. I can see all the appointments in bright red ink, as she continues sipping on a glass of red wine. I'd never seen her drink at all before this moment.

"Catherine, baby. Where did you see his backpack, sweetie?" My dad asks me, as I stare in silence at my mom. He steps in front of me, blocking my line of sight.

"Dad, I saw it in the attic window of Mr. Brittles' house. It's visible from the street. I noticed it after Meg, and I had a fight." I answer him.

He kisses my forehead, and then trots past me, grabbing his keys and heading for the door. My mother doesn't utter a word. She continues sipping her wine and staring down at her book filled with appointments.

I turn away from her to follow my dad and her words chill me to the bone.

"It's not Jack's backpack." She says coldly.

"What?" I ask, keeping my back turned toward hers. "It's not Jack's backpack in his window."

"How do you know?" I ask her, as a horrible realization dawns on me.

The day of Jack's disappearance, she hadn't been home. She went to Crowgrove County for an interview, which is why she had been wearing the floral dress. All this time, she'd not once cried over Jack being gone. She'd simply set up her interviews and cooperated with the police. Anymore, she didn't seem sad that Jack was missing.

"Mom, oh god. What did you do?"

"Nothing. It simply isn't Jack's backpack, is all."

"How do you know?!" I probe her again, this time slamming the door shut and turning back to face her.

"Because I know my son and I know Mr. Brittles. If he had taken Jack, do you really think he would've left evidence visible from the street? Especially with all the recent media attention Jack's disappearance has brought to this town. You're smarter than that Cat." Her mother says as a malevolent grin comes across her face.

"What did you do to Jack?" I ask her again, slamming my hands down at the table.

I no longer recognize my mother. She looks as if she's possessed as she sits across the table from me. Her facade fades away. She is no longer the caring or wonderful mother we had always known.

All this time, she had known what happened to Jack. I could feel the cruelty radiating from her.

She knew what happened to Jack, or worse, she made sure something happened to Jack.

"I did nothing to that mangy, filthy little brat! But, oh I wish I would have! Maybe then your father would care about me! Instead of about Jack!" she yells back at me, pushing her seat out from the table and stands up.

She flails her arms across the table knocking the wine and planner off the table to floor. As the glass shatters, she continues to shout at me.

"You were supposed to be the only child, Catherine. After you, I didn't want another child. But your dad has always been so pushy about everything. All his wants and his needs and his desires! Never considering yours or mine! But you were perfect, Catherine. You were healthy in all the right ways, and you were such a delightful baby. Despite how much I loved you and wanted you, for whatever reason. Your father couldn't attach to you, and I couldn't understand why. He never held you, never rocked you or carried you to your bed when you slept. I watched as you grew from an infant into a toddler, pining for his attention."

She lunges toward me, and I step to the side, avoiding her. I try to run away from her, but she grabs by my wrist and starts shaking me.

"You wanted your father constantly. No matter what I did, I couldn't make you want me or be happy with me! I tried so hard, Catherine! We went on walks together; I took you to the beach! On a girl's trip, just you and me! You were my everything. Yet, neither of us were enough for your father!"

She continues shaking me. I try to pull away from her grasp, but she continues to hold me and pull me closer to her.

"Mom, stop! You are hurting me!" I shout, trying to free myself from her grasp. She tightens her grip and forces me to look at her.

"After you, I was so tired, Cat. But, your father, he was going to leave us, and I couldn't pay for everything on my own. I had no money for daycare for you and I couldn't go back to work. I still had stitches in my stomach from my C-section. So, I came up with a plan." Her voice trails off as she releases me.

The moment she lets go of me, I stand there frozen like a statue, unable to move. My body shakes violently, but all I can do is listen.

"Jack, he was supposed to save my marriage, Catherine. Jack was for him, to make him stay! I gave him a son! A precious baby boy! Do you know what the worst part of it all Catherine is?" She asked me as she straightened her dress and wiped the corners of her eyes.

"What?" I question, though I feel as if I already know what she going to say.

"It worked. Your father he stayed with me, and you got to have your dad as emotionally neglectful as he still is. At least you got to have a father. We got to keep our home, our cars, and this entire world inside I created for you. For my perfect little girl. All I had to do was give your father a son." She finishes as she resumes her spot at the table, pressing her toes into the spilled wine on the carpet. Pushing the juice down until she hears a satisfying squelching sound beneath her feet.

"You never wanted Jack?" I ask her.

Thinking back to my childhood, as the pieces fell into place. Mom always lingering watching as Dad played solely with Jack.

She was always present but never took part in playing with him, or else Dad would snatch Jack from her arms. I thought they had just done that together playfully.

Now I know he'd done it because he had been afraid that she might hurt Jack. Or worse, that Jack may love her more. So, instead, he pushed away. Kept her away from him, despite how hard she wanted to be noticed by my father or have all she done for him acknowledged.

Dad never noticed mom or me, so we had each other. Mom would never hurt me, and he knew it.

"What did I need him for? I had you. You were mine. My mini me, aside from your traitorous eye color, which you inherited from him and his mother." She replies as she continues to press the stain further and deeper into the carpet. Never lifting her eyes back up to me.

"Mom, you are sick. Please, tell me where Jack is so I can get him some help." I say to her, trying to reason with her.

She cackles and throws her head back for a hearty, maniacal laugh.

"He's gone Cat. Didn't you hear? Poof! Gone! Vanished! Out like yesterday's old gossip column in the newspaper." She says, laughing as she flails her arms about to mimic throwing a bag out of a door.

Before resuming her former proper pose on the table. "Mom, can you please just tell me where he is?" I beg her.

She sits in silence, her eyes dart from a space on the ceiling to another space across the ceiling, looking everywhere and anywhere besides at me.

"Mom," I say again. "Mom please. He's just a little boy."

"Oh, Cat. He's gone. I don't know where he is. But if I did, I would tell you so you could bring him home and stop your dad from leaving us again. All this time, the only reason he's been here is Jack. He only loves Jack. He only loves the boys. You and I are nothing to him. Without Jack, there is no life here for us. He was talking about leaving next week, if Jack hasn't been found. I wish I had done something to him Cat because I'd return him. Safe and unharmed. Despite not wanting him, I have always loved Jack. A mother can love both, because she grows the babies inside her belly for 9 long months. She protects, feeds, and houses the babies. A mother's womb is a home and shelter for that child the moment it's conceived." She says as she sways back and forth.

She puts her face in hands and wails uncontrollably. I go to my mother's side and fix her hair.

"I'm sorry, Mom. I'll find Jack. I'll bring him home." Promising her, as I hug her tightly.

My mother's mental illness had been present since I was a young girl and though the whole family knew, no one ever told anyone outside of our household.

"I want him back. Please bring my baby back to me." She whines as she wails out in pain. I couldn't believe everything she'd just told me.

It was hard to listen to her falling apart and watching the sickness taking hold. In high-stress situations, the sickness always took over mom. She transformed into this violent, miserable, out of touch woman. All I could do was love her and watch over her through it all.

After putting my mother to bed and cleaning up the shattered wineglass on the floor. I finally left the house to follow my dad.

When I got to Mr. Brittles gate, it was open, and I knew I had to go inside. It was as if the open gate had been calling to me all along. The chain was gone and the padlock was missing. I tried to feel for it, in case my eyes were playing tricks on me again. But this time, it was gone. I saw my father's coat draped across the front porch banister.

He's probably already inside. Damn it, Dad. You should have waited for me.

Knowing I'd have to find out for myself, whether Jack was inside, and I'd finally uncover if all the rumors were true or not. I was the mouse in the cat's cage, this was his territory now. I took a deep breath, mustering up my courage.

"I'm coming, Jack." I whisper to the fleeting wind, praying that somehow my words would find their way to him and bring him comfort.

We were connected Jack and I, the way only a brother and sister bond could be. Something unseen, intangible, and unbreakable. Even when we are not together, I can still feel his energy, like a primal instinct, pulsating deep within the confines of my heart.

The moment I step inside the gate, someone grabs me from behind, pulling me backwards by the collar of my denim jacket. I spin around to see Dylan.

"Cat, are you crazy?" He asks me as crosses his arms over his chest. "You can't go in there."

"Dylan, buzz off. I am going inside." I tell him and turn back to the gate. He grabs my arm and when I try to pull away, he tightens his grip.

"Let go of me, you creep!" I demand, trying to jerk my arm free.

"I will not let you go in there. Cat, you do not know the monster that Mr. Brittles can be toward someone. You could get hurt, Cat." He tells me, finally releasing my arm.

I lunge away and take a step away from him. My face becomes hot, and I can feel the rage swelling inside.

"Dylan, I am going inside. Come with me or don't. I don't care. Jack might be in there." I say, my mind flashing with images of my little brother being tortured at the hands of Mr. Brittles.

Though I had never believed the rumors, I couldn't shake the feeling that something was wrong with Jack. My mind filled with images of him screaming my name and reaching out for me from a dark, endless abyss.

"No, Cat, you need to go home." Dylan tells me, stepping in between me and the gate, blocking my path. I see Jake and Megan running up the street in our direction.

"What's going on?" Megan asks us, as I ball up my fist, ready at any second to punch Dylan in the face and make him get out of my way.

"Dylan, man, what are you doing?" Jake asks Dylan. Still Dylan refuses to move, he shoves the gate closed.

"Jake, she's trying to go inside Mr. Brittles gates. The chains are missing, and so is the padlock. Someone must have taken them or something. I don't know where they are. But I had to stop her." Dylan explains.

Megan and Jake look at me, their eyes filled with fear.

"Cat, why on earth would you even think to go in there?" Megan questioned.

"You know why Megan. Jack he might be in there! I must go in there and save him. He's my little brother he needs me." I answer her, as I stare up at her face.

"Yeah, Mr. Brittles is dangerous. That's why this gate is here to begin with, to protect us all. Once you cross into his domain, that's it. You will never be seen again." Jake comments as he holds Megan's hand tightly, her fingers intertwined with his own.

"I don't care about some silly rumors!" I scream as I storm at Dylan.

Megan grabs my arm, pulling me back. Jake breaks away from her and steps in between Dylan and me. I break loose from Megan and lunge toward Dylan again.

"Get out of my way, Dylan!" I scream as my hands connect with Dylan's chest and he stumbles backwards.

"Megan, you better get your friend before she gets hurt!" Dylan warns.

Megan grabs me again; she holds me a little tighter as she pulls me away. Jake helps Dylan steady back on his feet as he pulls himself up, still holding to the gate.

"Megan, look, I know you like Jake and all that. But I am going over this gate. I saw Jack's backpack in the upstairs attic window. That is his hideous green backpack. I would recognize it from anywhere. I know he must be in there. Please, Megan, let me go." I tell her, she nods but doesn't move away from me.

"Cat, I know you really want to find Jack. Trust me, we all do. Jake and I have been up and down these streets all day looking for him. I've called out his name until my voice is hoarse. Cat, if he was in that house. He would've heard us calling out to him. But there's been no response or any evidence to suggest he kidnapped him. Not a whisper, or a whimper, or cry. It's like he just vanished from Bluebird Elementary." Megan says as she reaches out and pushes my hair behind my ear.

I see her look toward Jake, who has walked up the lane toward us now. I don't look at him, or at Dylan, who trails like a lost puppy following behind.

"Megan, I saw his backpack. Please, you aren't listening to me. I know what I saw. He's in that house Meg." I say with certainty.

"I can't explain it, but I know he's somewhere inside. Please, don't try to stop me." I tell her as I sprint toward the gate, running past Jake and Dylan.

They immediately turn to follow me; I see them do so from the corner of my eye. I don't look back; I run until I reach the gate. Pushing it open, I sprint to his front porch.

The moment my sneakers touch the front porch, I turn back to see Jake grabbing Megan, pulling her away from the gate. I can hear her calling out to me, begging me to come back. But Jake holds her firmly.

Her face is the last image I see before I turn back to the door. I pull it open, no longer hesitating, and step inside.

I'm sorry Meg, please forgive me.

One day you will understand why I had to do this alone. You are my best friend; I can't lose you too. Jack is my little brother, only I can find him. I must keep my family together.

The house is large and antiquated inside. Darkness clings to every surface in the entrance hallway surrounding me.

Only the light pouring inside illuminates the floor. I take a step further inside, as the uneasiness swells in my stomach, making me feel nauseous. The musky air has a sweetly rotten aroma pouring out of the vents.

I pull the door shut behind me, and instantly the darkness swallows me. I am like an unseen, quiet shadow as I navigate through the corridor, my hand clinging to the wall, trying to find my way in the dark.

My heart drums in my ears, my throat feels parched and dry, like it's cracking and bleeding from the crispness of the air. Silence looms like an unforetold secret from the halls, as I find the wooden banister in the dark and begin my ascension up the steps.

Megan should forgive me. I hope Jack's okay and I wonder if Dad's in here, too. I should look for him. But I can't call out to him. That would alert Mr. Brittles that I am in here too. I will try to find him and Jack while I am inside. Damn it, Catherine. You should've stayed with your friends. Instead, you're trapped in here with Mr. Brittles. If the rumors are true, you're as good as dead yourself.

I creep up the winding staircase quietly, trying to not make a sudden movement or sound. My heart pounds violently against my chest, and my fingers tremble with nervousness. I hear a cough come from the top of the stairs, and I instantly freeze.

I can feel someone's eyes on me and stand frozen like a statue as a dark silhouette stands atop the stairs. I squint my eyes, barely making out the outline of someone standing there in the dark.

"I know you're there." The words hurtle in my direction as if I am the rolling pins and they are a bowling ball.

They're fierce, sharp and shocking. I felt my knees wobble. I don't answer. As a mouse would, I stay as quiet as possible.

My mind retraces the memories and navigates through all the voices I've heard in town. None of the faces replaying like a film inside my mind match with the voice I've heard. Knowing it is a stranger and not someone I recognize sends cold shivers skittering like goosebumps across my skin.

"You are such a brave little mouse to enter the cage of a lion with an empty stomach and salivating mouth. You're the older Rhodes child, aren't you? Not the little boy, but the older girl. If he catches you, you won't be so lucky to get away, you know. Girls have more tender meat." The voice comes as a whisper, as a cool breeze as if someone unseen rushes by me, almost knocking me down.

I rest my weight against the banister, tightening my grip.

I hear it, the snap of the banister, and down I go. My body thuds hard against the cold tile floor before me, widespread pain floods through my body, originating from my ankle.

I reach down to touch it and a burning sensation hotter than hellfire shoots down my hip to the tip of my toes. As I lay there, I hear a door open upstairs and heavy thudding footsteps echo across the ceiling, making their way toward the stairs.

I have got to hide! It must be Mr. Brittles. He must have heard the commotion with the banister breaking, and now he is coming after me.

I wince as I crawl toward a nearby door under the stairs. Reaching up, I twist the knob and I pull myself inside, holding the doorknob shut just as I hear heavy footfalls on the staircase above me.

My mother's cautionary tale of events from when my grandmother had been a girl replay in my head.

"If you can't escape, you must hide." The heavy footsteps stop short of the door. I cup my hand over my mouth, trying to steady my breathing. Hoping with everything inside of me they won't hear me.

Who had been the voice and the malicious entity that flew past me and down the steps? Was it the spirit of one of the missing seniors who had lost their lives here? Or was it something else? Something much more sinister, an angry, lost soul looking for revenge?

My mind felt cluttered with thoughts, and the pain shooting through my leg was so intense, I knew I couldn't move it. I wondered if I'd die here too, as an eternally trapped spirit, like those who found themselves in this same room.

"Who are you?" A voice from the dark called out to me, from deeper within the closet.

Suddenly, they struck a match, lighting a candle. The light revealed a little boy with red hair and freckles. A kid like Jack. As I stared at his face, I came to recognize him.

The face in the darkness belonged to Charlie Planters, one of the missing kids from Crowgrove County.

"You're Charlie Planters, I recognize you." I say as the little boy crawls closer to me.

He scoots beside of me. His face is dirty, and his clothes shredded, as if he'd been attacked by a wild animal. Otherwise, he seemed to be uninjured other than maybe a little malnourished. His gaunt face gave away that it had been a while since he'd eaten.

"How do you know me?" He asked.

"I saw your photo. You went missing right after my little brother, Jack Rhodes, disappeared. Your parents have missing flyers posted all over Robin's Hollow. They've been looking for you, like my family and I have been looking for Jack." I answer, as I roll up the bottom of my jeans to examine my leg.

Bruising and swelling spread from my ankle to my knee, Charlie looked down at my leg as he pushed his glasses up on his freckled face.

"You're really hurt." He says as his little dirty fingers touch my leg, and I wince from the pain.

"Yeah, I know. Are there any other little kids in here like you?" I ask curiously. He shakes his head.

"I… I don't know. After he took me, I bit his arm and ran away. I've been hiding in here ever since." Charlie answers, as he pulls his small fingers away from my leg and touches his face.

"What are you doing?" I ask him as I roll my pant leg back down.

"You are warm. I've been so cold since I came inside this closet." He says as he coughs. I can tell by his appearance he doesn't have long left; his skin appeared tight like the skin of a drum.

His fingernails and toenails look thin and brittle, his bare feet and legs covered in hefty black powder like he'd at some point been rooting around inside a chimney.

When he spoke, his voice came out in hoarse whispers, and I could nearly hear his throat cracking from dryness with every word he spoke.

"We have to get out of here. You need to get out of here and go get some help." I tell him, knowing that my ankle is more than likely broken from the fall.

"I can't leave! He will catch me! And then he will do with me what he did to Sarah and the other kids!" He says, withdrawing from me and crawling back into the darkness.

"Wait! Please, Charlie, what happened to Sarah and the other little kids?" I ask, grabbing his hand and pulling him back to me.

I wrap him in a warm hug, desperate to not be alone. As his body warmed up, I held Charlie for a few minutes of silence. He hadn't been lying. His body felt like a block of ice and his hands and feet were filthy, as were his clothes. Still, I held him the way I used to hold Jack when he fell asleep on the couch and needed carried to bed.

"When he catches them, he takes them down to the basement. I… I followed him one time, when he got Sarah. She's my big sister; we'd been walking home together when he had taken us." Charlie whispered to me.

"Mr. Brittles, how did he get you? I thought he was bound here, locked inside his gates?" I ask him, as I move the hair out of his eyes.

He and his sister Sarah were the only siblings that had gone missing together. The article had told their ages, Sarah, 11 years old and Charlie, 4 years old.

Jack had just turned 5 years old when he disappeared.

The stench radiating from him made me sick to my stomach, but I knew he needed to feel safe, and I needed his help if we were going to get out of here alive.

"Not Mr. Brittles, the other man." The blood in my body ran cold.

I swallowed hard. Biting the back of my lip, as the thought of the haunting voice I'd heard echoing from the top of the stairs came flooding back into my memory.

"The other man?" I asked as my throat continued to tighten, my body trembled, and I released him from my grasp.

My mind drifted to the malevolent entity that had run by me on the staircase moments earlier, causing me to trip and fall.

"Mr. Brittles isn't the only one in here. The other man in here he's meaner than Mr. Brittles, he is the man that comes in the darkness and sneaks up on you like a cat ready to pounce at any moment." Charlie whispers between the sputtering of coughs and sneezes.

He slowly crawls further back into the darkness.

"Charlie! Wait, please!" I pleaded with him as I pointed to my injured ankle.

Charlie stops crawling. He neither continues nor crawls away. He sits up on his knees patiently, a look of dread spreads across his face.

"Tell me more about the other man, also Charlie. I need your help." I instruct him as I point at the direction of the doorknob overhead. He shakes his head.

"I don't like to talk about the other man."

"I know. But it's important that you do." I say, shifting my weight onto my other hip to take some of the pain from my leg.

"Why should I?" He questions as he picks at the scabs on his leg, scratching violently like a rabid animal at them.

"Charlie, your sister, and I need your help. Only you can do it. I'm banged up badly or I'd go with you. But you are our only hope." I reassure him.

"I need to know, because it might help me in my search for my little brother, Jack. He might be inside of here and I must find him. I saw his backpack upstairs in the attic." I say, trying to coax the youngster into more conversation.

He pauses, a puzzled look comes across his face.

"Is that why you came inside? To look for your brother?" Charlie asked me, his eyes filled with a dim light of hope, and I could nearly read his thoughts.

I wondered if that had been why Sarah got abducted that same day as Charlie.

If she were a sister like me; trying to protect her little brother, just as I had been trying to do with mine. A chill ran across my spine as I wondered if I would also share the same fate as Sarah.

That our brothers, Jack and Charlie, would somehow escape while we took their place instead. For that is what good sister's do, sacrifice and keep the younger alive.

Though by trading for their places, we undoubtedly could never leave from here. Remembered only as the young damsels who would become faceless, screeching, and haunted maids of the eerie little brown house at the end of the street.

We'd be forever cursed to haunt this tainted, wretched, and unholy ground. Our souls attached and chained to these walls. Despite how far we may go, we'd never get away from here. Our chains would always lead us back to this house, to the deepest part of the basements where he'd pluck the meat from our bones and we, just like the cautionary tale warned, would become boiled meat.

A feast for Mr. Brittles at last, on delicate girl meat. If our lives, would no longer be the same and if we too would stay trapped here with Mr. Brittles and the "alleged" other man for all of eternity.

If when we died here, that torment and tether would remain, and it would force us to be the prisoners of Mr. Brittles and his company for the rest of eternity. Though that might have been Sarah's fate, I am determined not to let it become my own.

"Yes, Charlie. I came here to look for Jack, just like Sarah came to protect you. Charlie, listen to me. Outside that door, my friends are down at the gate. If you leave this room, it is 15 steps in the darkness to the door. Only fifteen." I tell him, as I slowly arch the door open to sliver to peer out and look for any movement.

"I can't go. I'm scared. If I leave, he will get me. I know it." Charlie says in a whimper as he nervously looks through the crack.

"Please, Charlie. Listen to me, I'm too hurt. I can't make it. But you're smaller and you're faster. You are like a tiny little mouse, and you can make it to that door. I believe in you. You can make it out that door before he ever notices you." I encourage him, because I truly believe he can make it.

Because I know that if I can't at least get Jack out of here. I can save Charlie for at least Sarah's sake, and I hope she may do the same for me with Jack.

"What about Sarah? I can't leave her behind. She didn't leave me. It's all my fault that she is here." Charlie scoots closer to the sliver and I watch as he too peeks through the cracks.

We sit in silence, listening for footsteps. I strain my ears to hear, and I can hear the bubbling of a pot somewhere deep in the other side of the house.

"Charlie, the only way you can help Sarah now is by getting out that door and getting some help. If you make it out and make it to my friends, they can take you to the police station. Once there, you can bring the police back here. While you are gone, I will try to find Sarah and Jack. I will get them out too. But first you must go." I tell him, and I will try. However, I fear for his sister it may be too late.

I scoot away from the door, angling myself to where I can pull it open so that Charlie can get through and out that door. From where I sit, I can see the door. Fifteen steps for him to freedom. That's all it would take.

"I'm scared."

"I know. It will be okay. Just run as fast as you can."

"Promise?"

"Promise what, Charlie?" I ask curiously.

Assuming I'd already know, and the dread crept into my heart as I watched his mouth say the words that I knew he would.

"That, no matter what happens. You will save Sarah, too?" His eyes look up at me and I stare back down at his little face.

He looked so tiny, like Jack when he was an infant. In this cramped space, somehow Charlie looked even smaller. Almost as if he were visibly shrinking.

"Yes, I promise." It is the only lie that I tell Charlie, unsure if I can keep it.

But my words had been the fuel he needed, and he shot out of the sliver of the door in seconds.

The moment he pushed it open, a loud creak let out and I could hear the footsteps thumping through the house coming toward him.

"Run!" I screamed and Charlie makes it to the door. I watch as he struggles with the doorknob standing on the edges of his tiptoes to reach, and I scramble to my feet.

Standing in the open doorway, I scream again, distracting the thudding footsteps and I hear them turn coming toward me instead.

Charlie twists open the doorknob, and the light of early morning twilight pours in. Illuminating his body, he looks back at me for a mere minute.

"Run!" I scream out to him and as I hear his footsteps trot off the porch. I hear Meg and Dylan shouting.

"Oh my god, a kid just came out of the house!" Megan screams from outside.

Hearing her voice brings me the strength I need as I come face to face with Mr. Brittles, who smirks a sinister grin at me as he approaches me.

A long leather whip with metal hooks at the end clutched at his side. The moment my eyes see the weapon, my body kicks into action.

He is alone as he stomps toward me. I slip from the closet door and attempt to make my way up the stairs away from him.

"Holy shit, it's the missing kid Charlie Planters from Crowgrove County!" Jake shouts and as I head up the stairs I still a glance out the window to see Dylan hoisting Jake on his shoulders as he reaches down toward Charlie.

I continue to hobble my way up the stairs going as fast as I can, but I am not fast enough as Mr. Brittles gives chase from behind me.

"You can't hide, girl! This is my house!" He screams out as he slings the weapon toward me.

Somehow, I make it to the top of the stairs.

The moment I go to turn down the corridor, I feel the sharp sting of the blades of the hooked whip burrowing deep into my shoulder blade.

I fall and he drags me backwards, pulling my body toward him. I keep screaming and trying to scramble away, though my arms and legs feel like jelly, as if I had no bones.

One harsh flick of his wrist. I hear it snap behind me and I go down. My head catches the corner of the hallway table and I begin my descent into blackness.

The last thing I feel before I slip into unconsciousness is being drug backward down the steps. My head loosely bouncing off every step. I grab hold of the banister, but my grasp falls loose as my strength leaves me and my vision fades to black.

JACK

The day I went missing from the playground of Bluebird Elementary School feels as if it were a decade ago.

Before then, the rumors and stories of monsters were just that. Fiction and not reality, however, I would come to realize that some monsters, the actual monsters, are the ones that don't make the fiction pages. They're the ones we love, the ones we trust.

The ones wearing the skins of everyone we ever trusted, only to learn the truth that they are the most dangerous because they are the ones who birth us. They're the ones that feed us, clothe us and when we get too prickly or fat for their taste, they toss us out like trash into the bins.

My sister Cat and my dad they were the only safeguards I had against the monsters. But now, they're both dead. Leaving the actual monsters, the true monsters, a doorway of access that will lead them right to me.

That day at Bluebird Elementary, it was a shock to see my mother picking me up instead of my dad. After all, we all knew the dynamic in the household. Cat was her favorite, and I was Dad's.

I didn't want to get in the car with her. My feet had stood cemented to the sidewalk as I watched her roll down the window of the car.

"Jackie, get in! C'mon my sweet boy. We are going for ice-cream, you and I!" she said ecstatically as she sipped on her iced coffee and smiled.

Her makeup, and sunglasses and clothing were strange that day. Her face, something about it, just didn't look right. I knew from the second the thing pulled up; it wasn't my mother, it was just wearing her skin.

"I don't want to go." I remember telling my teacher as I fought to control my bladder.

The urgency to go was overwhelming, for I could truly see who it was.

The one part of the tale that I knew that no one else in town knew was that Mr. Brittles had been a shapeshifter.

I saw him take the form of an old black alley cat with piercing gold eyes. Once he had fully changed into a cat, I watched as he pounced up into the air, catching an innocent baby crow. When Mr. Brittles, in his cat form, carried his catch down the street.

My curiosity got the best of me and I followed him, wondering where he would lead me. The cat slithered through the iron gates, and I followed.

Secretly, slipping in between the gap in the gate. Once the cat went around the corner, I peeked from a nearby bush crouching down so he wouldn't see me.

There sat Mr. Brittles feasting on the same bird in his garden. It had only been a few days ago when I'd witnessed him change. His limbs elongated, his skin stretched, and as he yowled out loud, his gold eyes flickered back to human eyes.

What had once been a cat now had become a naked, wrinkly old man. I told no one what I saw, as I secretly crept back through the opening in between the gates. Immediately breaking into a sprint back toward my house, terrified I'd look behind me and I'd see him in that cat form or something worse following me.

Not even my parent's or my sister, or my teachers. But at that moment, I wish I had told everyone.

Maybe it would've changed everything for all of us.

Maybe they'd all still be alive if it weren't for my secrecy. I feared that they'd not believe me or say that I was making it up. A little boy with delusions of real-life monsters.

I knew about mom's illness, and I had overheard her and Dad talking about how the mental illness may carry down to either Cat or me.

That's why I didn't tell anyone. I was afraid they wouldn't believe me or accuse me of making up stories.

But, that night in his garden I'd witnessed Mr. Brittles change into the form of a cat, completely naked, devouring a small bird and walking around on his hands and feet with his back high in the air.

Arched just like a cat, completely nude. He'd done this for hours, and I didn't say anything. I just went back to my backyard, carrying his secret with me.

I'd snuck out at night without my parent's or my sister noticing. The blood dripped down the sides of his mouth, as the crows body crunches in his gnashing maw. He thrashes back and forth, blood spurting from his half open jaws.

I became disgusted at the display before me, and I could feel my stomach churning. I turn my head to a nearby bush and barf uncontrollably. I look back to see if he noticed me.

It was exactly as I feared, he was looking directly at me. His eyes peering into my soul. I immediately turned around and got out of there, praying he wasn't following behind me.

Mom and Dad thought I'd never left the backyard, but I had wandered down the street and back by the time they seen me swinging in the backyard.

I knew I couldn't tell anyone what I had seen or else I would be treated the same as Mom, crazy. I would have to be tested by doctors and given countless medicines to convince everyone else of my sanity.

I went limp in my dad's arms when he picked me up from out of the backyard swing and carried me inside and up to my bed to sleep.

His arms had always been the safest place to be, and when he held me, I felt untouchable as if nothing could ever hurt me.

That's how I knew that Mr. Brittles was impersonating my mother, and no one knew it was him other than me.

After witnessing him shape shift, so easily the way I had, there was no way I was getting in that car without a fight.

"I don't want to go." I told my teacher firmly, planting my feet in the playground mud.

If my teacher wanted me to go with Mr. Brittles, she'd best be prepared to catch me.

"Jack, honey, that's your mom. You need to get in the car." Mrs. Daniels told me.

I shook my head, backing away for her. Mrs. Daniels reminded me of an orange, not only by her scent but also by her size.

Her hair hung in twisted ringlets that draped down her back, decorated by a bright blue ribbon to match her dress. A plump woman with short legs and glasses that stretched to her forehead. Her dark skin reminded me of the sweet scent of coffee and cocoa in the morning.

My mother's favorite morning ritual was a chocolate candy bar in the morning with a steaming cup of coffee.

Sometimes, when she dropped me off, she'd let me have a sip of her coffee. Though her coffee was as blonde as the sunlight, filled with delightful sugars and cream. The mix with the chocolate had been such a treat for me. It was the one thing, the one secret, mom and I had. The coffee and chocolate bar, a tradition I feared that would never happen again.

"No!" I cried out as I ran away from her.

I could hear her panting as she attempted to chase after me. I climbed up the jungle gym, and I imagined as if I were climbing a mountain with slippery slopes.

Every time my foot or hand slipped, I regained my composure and pressed forward. Until eventually, I reached the top.

Mrs. Daniels had her hands on her hips as she stared up at me. Her long hair narrowly stayed in place with that ribbon, looking like at any moment the ribbon would burst.

"Jackson Rhodes, you get off of that right now and come down."

"NO! I am not going with her. She's not my mother."

"Jack, she is your mother. I've met her before, and I know what she looks like. Honey, that is your momma. I can't keep you here if she's here to take you home now." Mrs. Daniels replied, catching her breath.

I watched as she wiped the sweat from her forehead and glared up at me from underneath her glasses.

"Please, Mrs. Daniels. Can you just call my family? To check, I know she's not my mother. That isn't my mom." I insisted as I tightened my grip on the jungle gym, ready to hold on for dear life if she tried to pull me off of it.

Mrs. Daniels rolled her eyes and straightened her glasses. One hand still set on her hip.

"Jackson, that is your mother. I am not calling nobody. She's here to pick you up, and you got to go with her now. Honey, you must. If a parent comes to my door or out here asking for their child, I must give you to them. There is no point in calling anyone when I seen your mother myself, knowing she's here to get you." Mrs. Daniels told me as she reached out her hand toward me.

"Come on down, and I'll walk you to her car myself, Jack."

“She doesn’t seem different to you?” I asked her, doubting myself.

Wondering if maybe my paranoia about Mr. Brittles and his capabilities were getting the best of me.

Mrs. Daniels strolled a circle around the jungle gym. I could feel her eyes studying me, trying to figure out if I was right or not. She sighed and reached her hand out again.

“Your mother always seems a bit out of sorts to me. C’mon Jack, I’ll walk you to the car. You can go home, eat dinner, and do some homework. Then tomorrow when you come back to class, we will talk about this. I promise.” Mrs. Daniels said as I clutched her hand and allowed her to help me off the jungle gym.

I wish she would have listened, and that I wouldn’t have doubted myself that day.

But I just followed her quietly until I got up into the passenger seat and waved goodbye as the entity dressed as my mother pulled out of the parking lot and onto the main road.

It was just me and Mr. Brittles now. I could hear his skin tearing and ripping as he coughed. My mother's skin peeled away, and there sit Mr. Brittles behind the steering wheel.

"What do you plan to do to me?" I remember asking him.

"Everything." He answered and on that day I would learn the horrors and power behind that word.

Mrs. Daniels, why didn't you listen to me? If you had, you could have intervened. You could have saved me from a fate far worse than death. A fate in which now I am forced to recreate.

A darkness that I must purge from my body, and burn from my memories. A misery like mine doesn't go away with the day. It lingers, follows me everywhere, and when life gets too much, it whispers in my ear for me to end my life. To do it, and to stop being a coward. I want to bleed out the darkness from my body in the living room.

To slice my skin open and let the crimson flow. Sometimes I do, that's why I have these cuts all over my body. Sometimes, I burn myself with cigarette lighters and slice my skin open with the sharpest knives.

Just to see if I can still feel, cause after all the things Mr. Brittles did to me, it's hard to know if I am alive or simply a walking corpse. To be honest, I don't know if I am even human anymore, or if I like Mr. Brittles have become a beast with an unquenchable thirst for the blood of the innocents.

A few weeks after my disappearance, my dad and sister came looking for me. Mr. Brittles captured them both.

He dangled my father's lifeless body over an enormous, large boiling pot, twisting and turning it on the roasting rod until his flesh fell from his bones.

No matter how much he screamed or begged. Mr. Brittles wouldn't stop turning until the skin of my dad's flesh had been boiled by the steam. He'd been cooked alive, and I couldn't stop it. All I could do was sit in the closet with the gag in my mouth and my hands tied behind my back.

Forced to watch as he murdered him, and then ate the boiled flesh from his bones. He made a soup from his blood and ground up his organs. He cut his limbs apart with a bone saw and nibbled on one finger he'd cut off as you would an uncooked carrot.

The rumors had been wrong about Mr. Brittles having no teeth.

In fact, he had many sets of teeth. Custom made ones from sharks, and other various animals. One set of dentures had canine teeth, one set had shark teeth, and one set had feline teeth.

Whichever one fit the occasion is the one he would wear for dinner as he chowed down on my father's flesh and many others as well.

Packing the rest of his ground up portions of meat into clear plastic baggies and storing them in a deep freezer, he kept across from the enormous pot.

The more I cried and begged for him to stop, the more kids he killed and the more he ate of them. Never seeming to grow full or tired.

I'd fall asleep in the closet in urine stained shorts, from where he refused to let me out to take me to the bathroom.

Often, he'd attempt to feed to me portions of the missing kids he'd cooked or of my dad. When I refused to eat, he'd hit me or shove spoonful's of the meat into my mouth until I vomited.

However, what I didn't vomit, I had to swallow.

The same day Mr. Brittles had captured my father, my sister also broke in. Unlike my father though, she'd somehow sent a message to the outside world, and the police stormed into Mr. Brittles house.

It took 22 bullets to maim Mr. Brittles even after he had fallen; he continued to hiss and swat at the police officers. As he dragged his body across the floor, toward the closet, I set inside.

"Help!" I squeaked out, my voice hoarse from no water.

Despite my voice being so low, the police officer heard me. In Mr. Brittles' house, they found over 100 missing children's posters and several skeletons. Identifying the bodies and the kids would be no simple task.

Still, because of Catherine's rescue of Charlie Planters.

I was alive.

My sister was a hero.

Officers got me out of that closet and took me outside of the house. They also found Sarah Planters, who, though very emaciated, was still alive. He'd been peeling the skin from the back of her legs and consuming it.

She was tender and sweet like a pie, she'd been his "desert girl," she revealed in her statements to the police. Her body lotion had fragranced her skin, to a flavor Mr. Brittles had delighted in tasting. He'd allow her one rest room break a day, and to apply it. He'd occasionally feed her. A treatment far better than the one I received.

She'd told them he had told her skin reminded him of candy and tasted sweet, and because of that, it was the only reason she'd been kept alive.

The police found a few other missing children that had been hiding in closets or buried deep inside the confines of his walls. Alive, but all very emaciated and dehydrated.

Despite my hopeful wishes, they did not find Catherine. I am unsure of what happened to her. None of the meat found in his refrigerator belonged to Catherine. Nor had the police ever found her body, though they assume she's dead.

After we were all rescued, many parents moved out of Robins Hollow looking to take the surviving children elsewhere to start a new life. But my mom refused to leave Robin's Hollow.

She continued to fight every day for justice for me and Cat; it was her inability to relent that caused the prompt conviction of Mr. Brittles.

Mr. Brittles had a trial, and we all got to speak to the monster who destroyed our families, and everyone wanted him convicted.

However, without Catherine's body or confession, and with little to no DNA linking him to the other children. It seemed impossible to get a verdict.

The testimonies of the survivors confirmed a lot. However, other than I, no one else had seen him cook or eat other victims. His lawyer had attempted argue that my statement's couldn't be trusted and that the trauma I had endured had botched my memories of the actual events that occurred.

Still Mr. Brittles received a sentence many thought was unfair. He'd been gifted "life without the possibility of parole" in prison. He'd escaped the claws of death, despite how many lives he had taken.

For 20 years, my mother and I have wondered what had become of my sister Catherine. She refused to move from this town, though my therapist begged her to.

"Not until Cat comes home." That was always her response, and she meant it.

Until we knew what happened to Catherine, she'd not leave this town. So, it forced me to grow up here. Forced to walk by that house and gaze upon it, it's massiveness and colors attempting to lure me back inside.

Forced to see it when I came home from school and forced to witness as someone new moved in and fixed it up. Almost I felt like they did it in a mockery of what had happened to the other kids and I.

I got to grow up and Cat would remain a fourteen-year-old girl forever.

Her actions saved so many of us and we all got to grow up. But Cat, remained trapped as a memory.

To this day, no one knows what happened to Cat or if she managed to get away.

Her friend Megan, and her grandmother helped take care of me until I become an adult. My mother's mind was never the same once Cat didn't return home.

I have called Robin's Hollow Police department many times, insisting they open the case file for Cat or take another look at that house.

I have been on the blocked call list for over a year now, though I have many cell phones. Every time I get a new number, they're the first ones I call.

They have answered none of our questions, no one knows, and despite my mothers' best attempts, no one will give us answers about what happened to Catherine.

Though she encouraged the police department and the public, no one will burn down Mr. Brittles house at the end of the lane.

Despite the protests of the townspeople, his home has become a popular tourist attraction and destination spot.

The newest owner, Mr. Archer Skinner, a rumored relative of Mr. Brittles, has turned the place into a place that is to be loved instead of feared. I have asked him if he has uncovered any of Cat's things.

He assured me he has not, still my dreams tell me otherwise. Sometimes in my dreams, Cat comes to me in her school uniform and double ponytails.

She laughs and sits at the bottom of my bed, and then she takes my hand and lures me to the iron gates, inviting to come back inside.

To come and see her. That she is so lonely cooped up inside that big old house.

I tell her I can't and that she needs to move on and be free. She only grows quiet and disappears afterword's I wake up.

And there is no Catherine, no ghosts, or mischievous laughter, only the emptiness of the cold dark room.

For 20 years, I haven't stepped foot back inside that house.

But today, something different happened. As I went by Mr. Brittles house, I saw Cat standing in the attic looking down next to my lovely green backpack.

My dad was standing behind her with his hand on her shoulder. Both smiled down at me from the attic window and waved at me.

Just as I wave back, a sickening feeling hits my throat as I see Mr. Brittles sitting there in his rocking chair. Grinning at me as he takes on the faces of my dad and of Catherine, all a ploy to draw me closer.

My mother died today, unexpectedly from a heart attack, and all the hurt and pain led me back here to these gates. She told me she'd seen Catherine outside, and when she went outside, Catherine was gone. But a strange black cat sat in our yard with the largest yellow eyes she'd ever seen.

This was moments before death took her from this world.

Had Catherine become a shapeshifter and came to visit our mother on her last day?

Or had Archer Skinner had the same wicked ability as his beloved uncle, Mr. Brittles?

All these questions I worry about will remain unanswered. Somehow, Mr. Brittles escaped from prison and returned to his home.

I am thinking of going and asking him directly what happened to Catherine. I leave my house wearing a brown coat, boots and a gray beanie with matching gray gloves.

I have a gun stuck in the back of my pants, and today I will get the answers of where my sister is.

Though I think I already know, she's imprisoned somewhere inside bones of that house like my father.

An infinite prisoner unable to escape. Not even her soul can rest.

I go down to the end of the lane and see Mr. Brittles sitting in his chair with Archer sitting on the other side of the porch.

"Nice to see you again Jackie." Mr. Brittles says as he licks his lips from his rocking chair. Archer sits beside his uncle; he wears the face of my father.

My father's eyes stare in bewilderment at the object in my hand. Wide and terrified for the first time, with fear. Archer knows what I've come here to do today. He looks toward his uncle. Then his eyes meet mine, the smile from his face drops.

"I'll see you both in Hell." I tell them. I approach the gates; I lift the gun and fire.

Manufactured by Amazon.ca
Bolton, ON

56164435R00059